Spaceports & Spidersilk

February 2025

Edited by
Marcie Lynn Tentchoff

Spaceports & Spidersilk
February 2025
Edited by Marcie Lynn Tentchoff

All rights reserved. No part of this publication may be reproduced or transmitted in any form or by any means, electronic or mechanical, including photocopying or recording or by any information storage and retrieval systems, without expressed written consent of the author and/or artists.

All characters herein are fictitious, and any resemblance between them and actual people is strictly coincidental.

Story and art copyrights owned by the respective authors and artists
Cover art "Cat Spells" by Barbara Candiotti
Cover design by Laura Givens

First Printing, February 2025

Hiraeth Publishing
P.O. Box 1248
Tularosa, NM 88352
www.hiraethsffh.com
e-mail: hiraethsubs@yahoo.com

Visit www.hiraethsffh.com for science fiction, fantasy, horror, scifaiku, and more. While you are there, visit the Shop for books and more! **Support the small, independent press...**

Stories

12	Valaxian Bakeries Contest for Budding Space Cadets Award by William J. Joel
18	The Haunted Classroom by William Shaw
30	The Right Side of the Road by Lydia Volokh
44	Boots by DJ Tyrer
55	Space Station Zero-G by James Fitzsimmons
67	The Field Trip by Ellie Murphy
80	Thaw by Alex McNall

Poetry

29	Familiar Moon by Greer Woodward
36	Tanka by Lauren McBride
38	The Space Creature Crew by Guy Belleranti
39	A Dragon's Allergies by Brian Rosenberger
40	A Dog's World by Lisa Timpf
54	Before Plants by Jamie Manias
71	Wicked Woods by Leigh Therriault

Illustrations

39	Dragon Reading Material by Lisa Timpf
41	Renfield by Michelle St. James
85	Who's Who

SALE AT HIRAETH PUBLISHING!!!

BUY ALL THE BOOKS YOU WANT AND USE THIS 20% DISCOUNT CODE: BOOKS2024

GO TO OUR SHOP AT WWW.HIRAETHSFFH.COM

NO MASKS, NO WAITING, AND WE NEVER CLOSE!

What?

You don't have a subscription to Spaceports & Spidersilk???

(*Gasp*)

We can fix that!
Just go here and order:

https://www.hiraethsffh.com/product-page/spaceports-and-spidersilk

From the Editor

Greetings, readers, and welcome to the February 2025 issue of Spaceports & Spidersilk.

There's an old saying you might have heard at one point or another, that "the grass is always greener on the other side of the fence." It usually refers to the fact that, while it is easy to assume that others have less issues, or are happier than you are, that might not always be the case. It is always easy to see what is hard, or sad about your own life, and more difficult to think about what might be going wrong for others.

But being jealous because we can't see the obstacles that others face is all too easy.

This issue of Spaceports & Spidersilk is chock full of creatures with problems. Some of those problems are physical, such as a terrible injury that seems unlikely to heal, or an acute (and dangerously flame inducing) allergy. Some are environmental, dealing with a shifting or oddly transformed world. Some are caused by interference from outside entities, such as a too-controlling computer, or people intent on causing harm. And some are internal and emotional, like the need to prove oneself one's peers, or even more importantly, to oneself.

I think, in the end, all beings have troubles to deal with. The best we can do, as people, is try to work through our own, ask for help when we need to, and offer help when we can.

And, of course, since Spaceports & Spidersilk features stories and entities from various strange worlds, times, and dimensions, we *know* that the grass on the other side is very likely not to be greener than our own. In fact, it may well be pink, teal, or rainbow colored... maybe plaid? And that means we may still have reason to be just a *bit* jealous.

Happy reading!
Marcie Lynn Tentchoff

Pyra and the Tektites
Aquarium in Space

Pyra, age thirteen, is running away from home in the Asteroid Belt because she's not doing well in school. Her parents want to send her to Mars for school, and she doesn't want to go. She sneaks aboard a cargo shuttle, and falls asleep in the hold. When she awakens, she finds herself in free-fall; the shuttle has been seized by the Tektites, a group of rebel pirates . . .

. . . and the adventures begin!

Order a copy of the first book of this thrilling adventure series here:

https://www.hiraethsffh.com/product-page/pyra-and-the-tektites-1-by-tyree-campbell

Adopted Child

By Teri Santitoro

Imp, now 13, has awakened from stasis by MA, the ship's computer, to find that everyone else has been killed by a highly infectious disease. She is alone on the ship. But she is about to have visitors.

The *Greentown*, a salvage ship, has spotted a derelict and is about to board her for salvage rights. The crew is blissfully unaware of what happened to the people on the derelict. Soon enough they will find out...but will it be too late? And what of the girl who now controls the derelict?

To everyone involved, everything is new... and potentially lethal.

Ordering Link:

https://www.hiraethsffh.com/product-page/adopted-child-by-t-santitoro

Valaxian Bakeries Contest for Budding Space Cadets Award

William J. Joel

Rochelle was sitting at her computer, desperately attempting to complete a mountain of homework, when she heard someone knock on her bedroom door.

"Who is it?" she cried out, annoyed at having been interrupted.

No answered. Then she heard someone knock on her door, again.

"I'm busy!" she yelled. "I'm writing an essay for my history class so, whoever it is, go away!"

Yet another knock.

Rochelle pushed back her chair and stood up. She stomped over to her bedroom's door.

"This had better be good," she said.

Rochelle opened her door and stared at ... nothing.

"Okay," she said, "very funny. Ha, Ha. Whoever you are ..."

From below, she heard a tiny voice.

"Greetings, Earthling!" said the tiny voice. "It is my pleasure to inform you that you have won First Prize in the Valaxian Bakeries Contest for Budding Space Cadets!"

Rochelle shook her head and looked down to see a very, very tiny person staring at her.

This tiny person was holding out its hand and smiling at her. Rochelle blinked several times.

"Who," she said, "or what are you?"

The tiny person nodded its head.

"My sincerest apologies, Rochelle Stein," said the tiny person. "My name is Arkhghhdsjkll."

Rochelle's eyes open wide.

"But you can call me Fred," it said.

Rochelle blinked three more times.

"Fred?" she said. "What are you? And what the heck is this Space Card …"

"Valaxian Bakeries Contest for Budding Space Cadets," Fred interrupted.

Rochelle sighed.

"Whatever. What are you and what is it?"

Fred rubbed at his chin as if deep in thought.

"Well," he said, "the Valaxian Bakeries Contest for Budding Space Cadets Award is given each galactic year to a young individual who the judges feel would make an excellent candidate for the Space Cadet Academy."

Rochelle raised her left eyebrow.

"Academy?"

Fred nodded his head.

"Precisely!"

Rochelle rubbed her chin as if she were deep in thought.

"And," she said, "exactly how did I get this award?"

Fred laughed.

"Why," he said, "the essay you entered was deemed the best from out of over five hundred thousand entries, galaxy wide."

This time, Rochelle blinked four times.

"Err," she said, hesitantly, "I don't mean to be mean or anything, but I never submitted an essay to your competition. I mean, I'm honored to be awarded this ... honor ... but I think you've got me mixed up with someone else."

Fred shook his head.

"Impossible!" he said. "Our process is quite thorough, and we double ... no ... triple check everything before we award our prize."

Rochelle laughed.

"Well, perhaps you needed to check some more," she replied.

Fred thrust his tiny hands on his tiny hips.

"Your name is Rochelle Stein, yes?" he asked.

Rochelle nodded her head.

"And you live at 123 Main Street, Grand City?"

Rochelle nodded her head, again.

"And your parents' names are Arthur and Agnes?"

Another head nod.

"And ..."

Fred stopped asking questions and removed from his tiny pocket and even tinier device which he raised to his tiny ear.

"Yes? This is Arkhghhdsjkll," he said. "What? You did what? You sent me to the wrong planet? But? But? Yes, I understand.

Yes, I'll head for the coordinates you're now sending me. Thank you."

Fred replaced the tiny device in his tiny pocket. He then looked up at Rochelle and gave her a very tiny, weak smile.

"Ms. Stein?" he whispered. "There seems to have been an error."

Rochelle tilted her head to the side and grinned.

"Error?" she said.

Fred gulped.

"Yes, error," he replied. "It seems that somehow your name, address, etcetera, got substituted for the actual winner information. The true winner of the Valaxian Bakeries Contest for Budding Space Cadets Award is a young Zerbite on the other side of the galaxy. My deepest, sincerest apologies for having interrupted you, and raising your hopes of having won."

Rochelle grinned.

"I never entered," she said.

Fred cleared his throat.

"Yes, well, of course, you never entered," he said. "That said, if you will excuse me, I need to travel to the planet Zerbia to announce the award to the true winner."

Rochelle shook her head.

"And you're absolutely sure you have the correct information this time?" she asked.

Fred stood stiffly as if at attention.

"Yes! Absolutely!" he said. "Without a doubt. Fool me once, shame on you. Fool me twice, shame on me."

Rochelle smiled.

"Wait right here," she said.

Rochelle returned to her desk and picked up her smart phone. Then she went back to where Fred was still standing.

"Fred?" she said. "Can I take a picture with you, to prove I was visited by an extraterrestrial?"

Fred shuddered.

"What?" he blurted out. "I never! The indignity of the idea!"

Rochelle smiled.

"Well, if you don't," she said, "then the press might get a message from someone, like me, about someone, like me, who was incorrectly told she had won the Valaxian Bakeries Contest for Budding Space Cadets Award. I wonder how that would affect your career?"

Fred shuddered, again.

"You wouldn't," he said.

Rochelle gave Fred a very, large smile. Fred gulped, again.

"Fine!" he yelled. "Fine! Just one picture. But then I really do need to go."

Rochelle reached down and picked up Fred.

"What are doing?" he cried out.

Rochelle placed Fred on her shoulder, then lifted her smart phone.

"Say cheese," she announced.

Rochelle pressed a button on her phone which caused her device to both flash brightly, and take their picture. Fred rubbed at his eyes.

"Ow!" Fred screamed. "You could have warned me!"

Rochelle giggled.

"Sorry," she said. "don't they have devices like this where you come from?"

Fred sighed.

"Yes, yes, they do," he replied. "Now, I truly must leave."

Fred stood up on Rochelle's shoulder and pressed a button on his belt. As soon as he did, Fred disappeared. Rochelle stared at her now empty shoulder.

"Humph! Such a very strange person," she said. "I wonder …"

Rochelle lifted her smart phone and pressed a few buttons. She smiled when she saw the picture of her with Fred sitting on her shoulder.

"No one is going to believe this photo is real," she said. "But I know it's real."

Rochelle turned off her smart phone, closed her bedroom's door and returned to her desk.

"Now, time to finish off that essay."

Rochelle had just started to type when she heard a knock on her bedroom's door.

The Haunted Classroom
William Shaw

School wasn't going to be on the computer any more. For Susan and John Woodhouse, this came as a mixed blessing. On the one hand, it meant they would get to see their schoolfriends in real life again, and to play in the playground once lessons were finished. On the other, it meant they could no longer turn down the volume when class discussions got too loud, and there would be no more banana bread during school hours. But most of all, for Susan and John Woodhouse the return to in-person schooling meant this: the man they had so far known only as 'Dad' would transform, for seven hours every day, into 'Mr. Woodhouse.'

This was the only name Susan and John were allowed to call him while he taught their Year Six class, and he made it clear that they could not expect preferential treatment. "When we're at school, I am not your father," he told them at the end of the summer holidays. "At school, my name is Mr. Woodhouse. I'm a teacher like any other, and the two of you are students like any other. St. Chad's Primary School is my alma mater, and I want us all to do it proud."

"Dad, what's an armer martyr?" asked John.

"Don't call me 'Dad,' when we're at school," said Mr. Woodhouse.

"Sorry, Mr. Woodhouse," said John.

"We're not at school right – oh, forget it," said their father. "Just make sure you call me Mr. Woodhouse when we're at school."

Later, Susan looked up the phrase 'alma mater' on the internet. She learned that it meant 'nourishing mother,' which confused her, as she saw her paternal grandmother at least twice a year, and she was distinctly not a primary school. She went to ask her father about this, and found him sitting at the kitchen table, looking at his laptop. His eyes were oddly shiny.

"Mr. Woodhouse?" she asked.

Her father whipped round at the sound of her voice. He slammed the laptop shut, but not before Susan made out the logo of St Chad's Primary school, along with the words beloved colleague Margaret Milne and complications of COVID-19.

"Susan! You don't need to call me that when we're at home. How can I help you?" His eyes still looked shiny, and he dragged his sleeve across them in the way he was always telling Susan and John not to do. Susan decided to let it slide, just this once.

"I was wondering – Never mind. It's not important."

"Well, if you're sure," her father replied. "Are you all ready for the start of school tomorrow?"

"Yes," said Susan. "Are you?"

"Good question," said her father. "I think I'm as ready as I'll ever be." He stared into space for some moments, before adding:

"We're all going to have to be very brave, Susan. Remember that."

Susan said she would, and left her father alone with his thoughts.

***

Mr. Woodhouse maneuvered the family car into the school car park. He turned off the engine and twisted round to face Susan and John in the back seat. The children braced themselves. It looked like it was time for one of Dad's speeches.

"I know it's hard to be starting a new school year in these difficult times," he began.

Susan and John nodded gravely. Their father often talked about these times, which were variously uncertain, unstable, and unpresidented. Whenever these times came up, the children found that nodding gravely was the safest thing to do.

"We've all been through a lot over the past two years. But I'm so proud of you both for sticking it out, and for being so good about attending Zoom school while I was finishing up teacher training."

Susan and John nodded again, though Susan reflected that, really, their father had just been attending a different kind of Zoom school.

"Now we're all back in the classroom, I want you to apply yourselves just as hard as when we were at home. Year Six is an important stage in your school careers, and between you and me –" Mr. Woodhouse gave a theatrical glance from side to side. "I didn't do too well at it myself."

"Really?" said John.

"But don't you have to be clever to be a teacher?" asked Susan.

Mr. Woodhouse laughed. "Oh, it's not that I wasn't clever. I thought I was the cleverest boy in the world. I just didn't try. I'd done so well in Years One to Five, I thought I didn't need to. I drove my poor teacher mad. I would never remember the things she tried to teach me, and it was only much later that I realised what a fool I'd been."

Mr. Woodhouse stared mournfully at the school buildings for a moment, before appearing to rally himself.

"So I want you both to promise that you'll do your best this year, not just for me, but for yourselves. You only get one go at Year Six, like with most things in life. You have to make the most of it."

"Yes, Dad," said Susan and John.

"Yes, Mr. Woodhouse," said Mr. Woodhouse.

***

The bell rang for the start of the school day, and Susan and John filed into their classroom. They sat down together in the front row, next to their old friend, Dean Thompson.

"Did you hear that the school's haunted?" said Dean.

Dean had been a friend of Susan and John's since Year One. He was a big kid, with close-cropped hair and a chip-toothed grin. Susan and John had missed him while they were doing Zoom school, but Susan had not missed his tendency to believe everything he heard.

"No way!" said John. "The school's haunted?"

"I agree," said Susan. "There's no way the school is haunted."

"It is, too!" said Dean. "Brian told me! You know his Mum is one of the cleaners? Well, she said she was in here over the break, and she heard a voice from nowhere!"

"What did the voice say?" asked Susan.

"Open your books at page 23," said Dean.

"Not a very scary ghost, then," said John.

Dean went pink. "Well, she only heard it for a minute! I'm sure it'll say way scarier stuff if we just keep an ear out."

"What are you kids talking about?" asked Mr. Woodhouse, who had taken his place at the front of the classroom.

"Brian says the school is haunted," said John. "From the sounds of it, by the ghost of some old teacher."

Mr. Woodhouse's face went suddenly white, then red, then purple.

"That... is a very insensitive thing to say," said Mr. Woodhouse, quietly. "After everything the teachers here do for you, to treat their memory with such..." He tailed off.

"Is everything alright, Dad?" asked John.

"My name," said Mr. Woodhouse, "is Mr. Woodhouse! And since you're so fascinated with the supernatural, John, spell the word 'exorcise'!"

"Um," said John.

"'Um' is not a letter!" barked Mr. Woodhouse. "Now, spell 'exorcise,' while we're still young."

"E-X-E-R-S-I-S-E," said John.

"Wrong!" said Mr. Woodhouse. "Stay behind after class and write out the correct spelling a hundred times."

"But, Dad –" said John.

"My name is Mr. Woodhouse!" yelled Mr. Woodhouse. "While you're at it, you can write that out a hundred times as well. Now, I want you all to write two pages about 'What I did on my summer holidays' while I go and fetch your worksheets for our next lesson. If I hear a peep out of any of you, you will all be for the high jump."

Mr. Woodhouse stalked out of the classroom. Everyone else nervously bowed their heads in composition.

***

Susan had gotten as far as On the first day of my summer holidays, I... when she was struck by the futility of the exercise. What was the point of telling her father what she had done on her summer holidays? He already knew. And besides, most of the holidays had been spent on the sofa watching She-Ra and the Princesses of Power. She was staring into space, contemplating the problem, when she noticed something peculiar.

"The whiteboard!" she cried. "Look at the whiteboard!"

The whole class looked up, and there was a collective gasp of amazement. There, on the previously pristine whiteboard, dark letters were starting to appear. King George VI, they read. 1820-30.

"Something's writing!" said Dean.

"Obviously," said Susan.

"But what?" asked John. "I can't see anything doing it!"

The letters continued to appear. King William IV, 1830-37. Queen Victoria I, 1837-

"WHAT IS THE MEANING OF THIS?" thundered a voice from the other side of the room.

Mr. Woodhouse was back, and his face was redder than Susan had ever seen it. The writing had stopped the moment he walked back into the classroom.

"I told you all to stay in your seats!" said Mr. Woodhouse. "And I come back to find you've graffitied the whiteboard!"

"Funny kind of graffiti," said Susan.

Mr. Woodhouse rounded on his daughter.

"Silence!" he bellowed. "I will not tolerate this kind of insubordination! You can stay behind with John and copy out 'I must not perpetuate insubordination' a hundred times. Now if you're all quite finished, we can turn at last to mathematics."

The class groaned. Susan fumed. At the next desk over, she could see John trying to hide a smile. It was so rare for him to see his sister in trouble as well.

***

It was half past three. The rest of the class was gone; only the three Woodhouses remained.

"Right," said Mr. Woodhouse. "You both know what to do. I'll be at a staff meeting for the next hour, and when I get back, I want to see all those lines finished."

"Yes, Mr. Woodhouse," said Susan and John.

"Get on with it, then." Mr. Woodhouse slammed the classroom door behind him.

"This is so unfair!" cried the children.

"Life isn't fair," came a voice from the front of the classroom. "I'm afraid you must both learn to deal with it."

Susan and John looked up, astonished. Before them stood a tall, grey-haired woman in a floral dress, holding a whiteboard pen in her hand. She looked somehow faded, as if viewed through a dirty window frame. No doubt about it; she was a ghost. But, more worrying still, she was the ghost of a teacher.

"Now, as I was saying, Martin," the apparition continued. "I shall not rest until you can tell me the dates of Queen Victoria's reign! How are you ever going to become a successful adult without knowing something as simple as that?" She glared at John.

"M-Martin?" stuttered John. "But my name's not –"

"Do not contradict me, Martin!" barked the ghost. "Now, I want you to write out the dates of Queen Victoria's reign a hundred times. And you," she rounded on Susan, who flinched in her seat, "can start memorising the dates of the English Civil Wars."

"Yes, Miss," said Susan.

"That's Mrs. Milne to you," said the ghost of Mrs. Milne. "Now, both of you, get on with your work."

And so they did.

***

Forty-five minutes later, John politely raised his hand.

"Yes?" said Mrs. Milne.

"Please, Mrs. Milne, I've finished writing out the dates of Queen Victoria's reign," said John.

"Very well, Martin. What were the dates of Queen Victoria's reign?"

"1837 to 1902, Mrs. Milne," said John.

"1901! He means 1901!" said Susan.

"Yeah, that's right," said John hurriedly. "1901! I'm sorry, I couldn't read my own writing. Can we go now? It's getting on for dinner time."

Mrs. Milne gave a deathly smile. You might think it would be impossible for someone who was already dead to look even more deathly, but Mrs. Milne managed it.

"Oh no, no, no," she said. "I cannot rest, as a teacher, until I'm confident that you know the dates of Queen Victoria's reign, Martin. And since you're still so reliant on your classmates, I don't think you're quite at that stage yet. Now write it out another hundred times, and you," she turned to Susan, "can get started on the Glorious Revolution."

Susan and John looked at each other in despair.

"We're going to be stuck here forever!" whispered Susan.

"She's bound to run out of history eventually," said John, ever the optimist.

"Don't be so sure," muttered Susan. "New things happen every day."

John looked horrified. This evidently had not occurred to him. "What are we going to do?" he asked.

"I've got an idea," said Susan. "You know this used to be Dad's old school, right?"

"We can't call him Dad here!" said John. "It's Mr. Woodhouse!"

"Yes, John," said Susan, quietly. "Mr. Martin Woodhouse."

At that moment, Mrs. Milne materialised between them. "No talking in class!" she ordered. "Honestly, how on Earth do you expect to get ahead with an attitude like –"

There was a loud creak as the classroom door opened, followed by a yell of surprise, and the sound of several worksheets cascading to the floor. Mr. Woodhouse had entered the room.

"Mrs. Milne!" he exclaimed. "What are you doing here?"

"Martin Woodhouse!" exclaimed Mrs. Milne. "What are you doing here? And since when did you have access to the photocopier?"

Mr. Woodhouse looked sheepish. His eyes dropped to the ground, and he kicked his left foot nervously. The children stared at this transformation in their father.

"I- I- I'm a teacher now," said Mr. Woodhouse. "I was so looking forward to working with you. To showing you – What I can do now."

Mrs. Milne snorted. "You? A teacher? You can't even remember the dates of reign of Queen Victoria!"

"Twentieth of June 1837 to twenty-second of January 1901," said Mr. Woodhouse, automatically.

Mrs. Milne's eyes widened. Then she broke into a smile so bright Susan and John had to shade their eyes. "Well, I never," she said, softly. "Martin Woodhouse... ready to be a teacher."

"It was all your doing," said Mr. Woodhouse. "If I'd paid a bit more attention, I might have gotten here sooner."

"Well, you're here now, Martin, and that's what counts." Mrs. Milne turned back to Susan and John. "Class dismissed. Good work everyone. And Martin," she turned again to Mr. Woodhouse.

"Yes?" he said, looking hopeful.

"Good luck," said Mrs. Milne. "You'll have to be very brave. But I think you can do it."

And with that, the ghost of Mrs. Milne vanished.

Silence reigned in the once-haunted classroom.

Eventually, Susan ventured to speak. "Dad," she said. "That was your old Year Six teacher, wasn't it?"

"Yes," her father replied. "She taught me everything I know."

"Except for the dates of the reign of Queen Victoria?" asked John.

Their father laughed. "Except for those. Though not for lack of trying. Eventually, I grew up, and I learned them for myself."

"Does that mean she's gone now?" asked Susan. "She said she couldn't rest until she knew you knew them."

"I suppose so," said Mr. Woodhouse. "We've exorcised the ghost."

"Exorcised!" said John. "E-X-E-R-C-I-S-E-D!"

Mr. Woodhouse gave a small, tired smile. "Close enough, son," he said. "Close enough."

Familiar Moon
Greer Woodward

Whiskers whisper
  incantations
Gold eyes trigger
  transformations
Turns of earth
Twists of sky
Witches hiss
as black cats fly

The Right Side of the Road
Lydia Volokh - 12 years old

She wasn't programmed to feel emotions; neither was anyone else. Everything was answered with the most logical explanation. Everyone's life was set to a program. Her whole life was controlled by a computer screen on her chest. To the computer, every question had an answer, and that answer was the right one. Always.

Every day was the same. Every day was pre-decided. She woke up every day at the same time. She went to school every day at the same time. The computer would decide everything. The computer decided how hard she worked, whether she studied, and what grade she got (100, obviously). Every student had a different program. She was programmed never to stop working. She was as punctual as a star, at least, that's what the computer said she was supposed to be. Every day was the same.

At the end of the day, she would go home. Some students were programmed to "relax," but not her. She got home and she worked. She took care of her siblings as if they were her children. Her father was programmed to be a soldier in the Cyborg War. He wasn't here right now. Her mother's program broke years ago. She asked the computer how she should feel; the computer said she shouldn't. That was more efficient after all. After her mother's program broke, she learned one thing: Never be like her. If she disobeyed the program too many times, it would shut down. The program was life exactly how you were supposed to live it. The program was everything. If you didn't follow it, it would break. If it broke you would have too much control. If you had that control, you would face completion.

Civilians aren't supposed to know what completion is. That's the one question you can't ask the computer. All they know is that completion happens at the end of your life when you've finished your program. But sometimes (like with her mother) the police make you have an early completion. We don't know what happens after completion, they're just... not there.

***

It was what would have been November 16th, 4747, the day was going perfcctly: Just according to the program. She woke up at her usual time. She was on pace to arrive at school at the normal time. She turned a corner and asked the question that she asked every day at 7:16 am:

"Computer, which side of the road should I walk on?"

The screen showed the answer: "Left."

Why did it say left? It always says right. Why did it say left? The right side of the road is the right side of the road and the left side is the wrong side. Now the left side is the right side and the right side is the wrong side. She acted... against the code when the program wasn't the same every day. She didn't like change. But, she calmly walked over to the left side of the road the right side of the road, she reminded herself, left is right. Suddenly, she tripped, landing on her stomach.

She looked up "Computer, what should I do?" she asked.

No response.

She asked again: "Computer, what should I do?"

No response.

She looked down: Her computer was shattered, and only one word showed on the screen in response to her question: LIVE.

No, no, no, no, no, no, no, no, no, no, no, no, no, no, no, no, no, no, no, no, no, no, no, no, no, no, no, no, no, no, no, no, no, no, no, no, no, NO, NO, NO, NO! She couldn't be like her mother. She couldn't be. If the computer goes down then so does the program. If the program goes down then so does she. Nobody can know. She can't complete. She can't.

She covered up her shattered computer with her jacket. She needed to be her own computer. She calmly walked over to the right side of the road. The right side of the road is the right side, and nothing bad can happen on the right side of the road. The left side of the road is the wrong side of the road.

She arrived at school 2 minutes late. Nothing was according to the program; there was none anymore. She felt this sick feeling in her stomach. Strange, she wasn't programmed to be ill for... it doesn't matter anymore. Suddenly she was in her first class. Suddenly she had a test in front of her. Suddenly she felt that sick feeling. In the class Unprogrammed 101 they described this feeling that you could have when your system was broken: stress, it was called stress. She didn't like that feeling. She didn't like that feeling at all.

The test. She was programmed to have studied for this. The information should be in her system by now. She should be able to take this test. She should be able to ace this test.

D+. She got a D+.

"What is wrong with you?" The teacher asked.

What was wrong with her?

"System reboot" she lied.

She wasn't programmed to lie either. What was wrong with her? She had to move on from it. She had to be asking what was right with her.

It was recess. She could make it through recess... She definitely couldn't make it through recess. Another feeling that they talked about in Unprogrammed 101 was freedom. It was described as a sort of recklessness, and an urge to destroy, and disobey. She liked this feeling though. She wasn't supposed to, but she sort of liked being free from the reins of the program.

She didn't even try to ask the computer this time; she picked up a rock and threw it at someone's screen, just to see what would happen. She watched the screen on his chest shatter into a thousand pieces and fade to black. She saw it die–like hers did–as if it was trading its life for his. She saw him die inside, finally feeling that sick feeling that can only be compared to death. Immediately, teachers took him away to see if there was any hope of that screen being repaired, of course, there wasn't.

"No!" He screamed, "Don't take me!"

She saw him feel fear, real fear. Not the fear you were programmed to feel.

"It's only protocol." The teachers said as they dragged him by his arms. Resisting as if losing the program actually meant losing your life. Well, it did... because of the system. She saw the look on his face. You could feel it when you were past the point of no return, you knew, the voices just... stopped. Your mind went blank as the realization struck you, you just knew. The next day it was announced that he was scheduled for early completion. She did that to him, just another reason why nobody could find out about her.

***

People eventually started noticing. She kept getting in trouble, failing tests, acting out, and then chalking it all up to having a "short reprogramming" or a "system reboot". They sent her to the doctor, she was programmed to be a doctor, once upon a time. She tried to stop it. She tried to run, but they saw her screen eventually.

"NO!" she screamed, "NO!"

Getting caught meant reliving her mother's completion. She couldn't be like her mother. She realized this was the same thing that she put that kid through. But maybe it was worth that glimpse of freedom.

They tried to see if they could fix it. She tried to tell them that it just wasn't possible. They didn't listen. Nobody ever listens. They try to fix something that doesn't want to be fixed, that doesn't need to be fixed. They just needed to listen. They just needed to let her be.

They told her she had 3 days until her completion date. 3 days to spend with the people she "loved," as if they knew what love was. They haven't felt anything, they couldn't feel anything with that stupid program. They hadn't felt stress, or guilt, or anxiety. They hadn't felt betrayal, fear, or disappointment. They hadn't failed, questioned life, or tried to run. They hadn't held someone's life in their hands, they hadn't even held their own life. She wanted to show them so badly what it felt like to feel emotions. Just like she showed that kid, the kid whose screen she broke, the kid she showed freedom to. She didn't know what completion was, but she knew she wanted to feel instead.

***

She packed her bags and left. That was the only solution, she ran. She ran and ran, and ran. It used to be that with the program, feeling physically ill was scheduled. But now, she felt it in her run. She felt it in her step. She felt it in her throat, in her stomach, in her feet, and she liked it. It made her value the time when she felt her best.

There was nothing but cities for miles. She couldn't go to another city. Cities have programs. Cities have computers. Cities have everything she needed to escape from. She turned the corner. It's such a familiar question that she can't help but ask it:

"Computer, which side of the road should I walk on?"

She waited for an answer, she didn't expect one, but she stayed anyway. There was no answer, but she knew it already. She walked over to the left side of the road.

> missing
> new chef bot
> reorganized Mom's kitchen
> last told to
> get lost!

After Asimov's I, Robot: Chapter 6

Lauren McBride

Mellie

The Adventures of a Teenage Vampire

Meet Mellie, an adolescent vampire, as she travels to Italy and New York to discover roots, make friends, and of course get into trouble. Fun adventures for the whole family.

https://www.hiraethsffh.com/product-page/mellie-the-adventures-of-a-teenage-vampire-by-debby-feo

The Space Creature Crew
Guy Belleranti

My class soared by space bus
To meet the Creature Crew.
All three were amazing.
I think you'd like them, too.

The first creature was huge
With a crescent moon nose,
Flying saucer-shaped eyes
And long rocket ship toes.

The middle-sized creature
Had rings circling its head
In beautiful Earth blue
And marvelous Mars red.

The last was the smallest,
But my favorite by far.
Its bright sweet smiley face
Twinkled just like a star!

A Dragon's Allergies
Brian Rosenberger

If in the nostril, an itch
better run for the nearest ditch
Best sound the alarm
maybe hose down the farm
Watch the firemen scurry
always cause for worry
If a dragon should sneeze
Beware, an inferno on the breeze

Dragon Reading Material
Lisa Timpf

A Dog's World
Lisa Timpf

Each species tells its own stories
about the world and its meaning
and in the lore told by dogs
the moon and sun are giant flying discs
herded across the sky by border collies.
Clouds are clumps of mashed potatoes
always hovering just out of reach.

Lake-beds are the footprints of giant wolves,
filled, over time, by rainfall
and swift-flowing streams,
and puddles are nature's drinking bowls
regardless what one's master might say.

Rainbows offer a reassuring reminder
that even after a dreaded bath
the sun will come out again.

Renfield
Michelle St. James

New From Hiraeth Publishing!!
Cats and Dogs in Space
By Lisa Timpf

Cats in lab coats, running experiments on *us*. Robot dogs roaming Mars. Space-faring canines who mistake alien vessels for fetch toys. There are just some of the images you'll find in here. With inspiration from myths, news stories, nursery rhymes, personal experience, and a lifelong interest in science fiction, the poems are written in a variety of styles for your reading enjoyment. Reaching from the distant past to the far future, and points in between, *Cats and Dogs in Space* invites you to have some fun re-imagining man's best friend—and whatever it is that cats call themselves.

When we beamed the book to the future, here's what readers had to say:
"Purrfectly delightful! Enjoyable for readers of any stripe. Some of these poems are enough to make a cat laugh!" *Festus, ship's cat aboard the Silver Starr Spaceliner Frederika.*

"Meaty as a prime rib bone, and just as much fun to chew on! I'd give it two thumbs up—if I had opposable thumbs . . . " *Pepper, K-9 Operative, Galactic Space Services*

So there you have it! Get *your* claws on a copy today!

www.hiraethsffh.com/product-page/cats-and-dogs-in-space-by-lisa-timpf

Boots
DJ Tyrer

It all began in an inn, and ended outside of it on a chilly night. Not because that was where such adventures were supposed to begin, as old Tolomai always told her, but because that was where Cathy lived and she could never control her curiosity.

From the moment she first saw them from her perch in the rafters, where she was absently stroking white-footed Boots, Cathy was certain the pair, who had just entered the inn, were villains. The man was head and shoulders taller than her uncle, who was a big man, and had a thick black beard and arms that were hairy like a bear's. She was certain he was some kind of evil knight. The woman who was with him also had black hair, but with twin streaks of silver running through the freely-flowing tresses, and was wrapped in a dark cloak. She, Cathy thought, had to be an enchantress.

"Trouble," she told Boots. The cat purred in agreement.

The pair approached her uncle and asked for a room for the night. He delegated Tolomai to show them upstairs.

"We should keep an eye on them," Cathy decided.

That was easy enough. The inn was old and had plenty of spaces through which a cat, or a child, could crawl with ease, spying upon the guests staying there. Such spying was a habit with Cathy, and Boots was always with her as she watched.

So, after the maid, Kyla, had tucked her into bed, Cathy rolled back out from under the covers and summoned Boots from where he had been luxuriating beside the small stove that heated the room, and moved a stool so that she could clamber up atop her wardrobe and reach the space between the rafters in the wall above it.

Carefully, she picked her way between the cobwebs, sending spiders scuttling off into crevices in fright, and through the skeleton of the inn and made her way to the room where Tolomai had put the pair. She crept out onto a beam above their heads and listened.

"...then, our ally will unlock the door for us so that we can enter the palace unobserved," said the woman. "You remember the route?"

The man nodded. "I do."

"When we reach the Prince's chambers, I shall charm any guards. Once inside, you will kill him, and –" She fell suddenly silent and looked about. "Did you hear –?" She looked up – straight at Cathy! "A spy!" shrieked the woman.

Cathy almost fell from her perch in shock. Desperately, she tried to turn about on the narrow beam.

The woman's voice was quiet as she spoke again, her tone softened.

"Do not fear, little one. We mean you no harm. Jump down and receive a gift."

Cathy could see the man drawing a dagger from his belt, but thought nothing of it.

She swung her legs off the beam, ready to drop.

"That's it...good girl," crooned the woman.

There was a sudden raking pain and Cathy yelped. Boots had just swept his claws along her arm.

"Boots!" Then, she remembered the dagger. Without further thought, she pulled herself back onto the beam and began to hurry off after the cat.

"It's the innkeeper's child," Cathy heard the woman say as she slipped into a narrow space. "She's going nowhere. Find her and deal with her."

The man grunted an acknowledgement, and Cathy heard a door open and close.

Moments later, she dropped back down into her room, Boots hopping down beside her.

"Thank you," she said, knowing that, somehow, Boots had saved her.

Then, she looked at the door. It was bolted shut, but the little wooden bolt suddenly didn't look very secure when she considered the size of the bear-like man.

As if response to her thought, the door shuddered and she heard the bolt crack.

"What do you think you're doing?" she heard a low, whispery voice ask. Tolomai.

There was a brief sound of scuffling and a gasp, then she heard a thud.

"Tolomai?" she called.

The door shuddered again.

Boots tugged at her leg. Yes, she needed to get out of there.

She clambered back up into the rafters. She'd find her uncle; he'd know what to do.

Behind her, she heard the door burst open and the man curse.

As she climbed through the innards of the building, the night was no longer silent. There was a hubbub and, with it, the smell of smoke. The inn was on fire!

Cathy hurried along beams and through crawlspaces, smoke beginning to curl along beside her, panicking and no longer certain which way was which.

Boots tugged at her sleeve, guiding her.

There was a hiss, neither that of the cat nor of the fire that was spreading through the inn. From the darkness, a figure crawled towards Cathy, blocking her way – it was the woman. Though tall, she was slender enough to fit within the same tight spaces as Cathy.

Following Boots, the girl turned and scrabbled her way along a different route. He paused beside a small hole and nodded at it, as if to say 'This way, this way.'

This way was narrower and she could barely squeeze through.

A hand caught her ankle and pulled her back.

Cathy screamed and tried to kick backwards, but it was difficult in the confined space.

Then, she heard the woman shriek in pain and her ankle was released and she knew that Boots had saved her again.

With a powerful squeeze, she pushed on through and found herself on a beam above the main bar of the inn. Flames licked about the place and the doors were open, her uncle guiding guests out into the chilly night.

"Tolomai!" she heard him shout above the growing roar of the flames. "Cathy!"

Kyla came running. "I can't get upstairs. They must be outside."

Her uncle nodded and they stepped out of the building.

Cathy called after him, but the sound of the fire was too loud for him to hear her.

Tolomai... Was he alright? She was certain the big man had hurt him... was he dead? Or, was he laying there unconscious with the flames spreading towards him? She had to help him! Only...

There was the sound of crashing as something, a wall or the roof, gave way.

Terror flooded through her, just like the smoke was flooding through the building, making her cough.

But she couldn't just leave him.

"Boots, Tolomai," she managed to gasp.

The cat seemed to understand her and disappeared off along one of the beams, while she followed another towards the door.

It was becoming difficult to see, the smoke was so thick, but she was certain she was nearly there. The area nearest the door was still free of flames and she thought she could probably get outside if only she could reach it.

But, first, she needed to pause, rest – her limbs felt so heavy and weak...

Recovering a little, she pushed on, praying that Boots had reached Tolomai and that they were both fine.

Right, she had to be near the door...

She dropped down to the floor. It held.

A huge dark figure loomed up out of the smoke at her. It was the bear-like man.

"Got you," he cried with a cruel tone of success, grabbing her shoulders.

Then, he stiffened and his grip loosened, and he fell to the floor.

"What?" she cried.

Another figure appeared, a smaller and wirier silhouette with something square-ish in its hands.

"Tolomai!"

He dropped the chair he held and reached out for her hand.

"This way." He pulled her from the burning building and called out for her uncle.

As Tolomai explained in broken sentences what had happened and directed her uncle and some of the guests to drag the unconscious man from the bar room, Cathy felt a small shape push against her legs.

"Boots, you're alive!"

The cat purred at her. Then, it hissed.

The woman had stepped from the burning building, imperious in spite of the soot and cobwebs that smutted her shoulders and hair.

"That's her," shouted Cathy, although nobody had any reason to know who 'her' was. "She's plotted against the Prince and she started the fire."

The men who had rescued the big man and bound him with rope, looked at the woman in some confusion, then moved forward as if to detain her, too.

She raised her hand and they halted as one.

"Listen not to the girl. Seize her." Hands did. "Release my companion."

Groggily, the big man stood.

With a cruel smile, the woman told him, "Kill the girl and these fools."

"I'll start with the old man," he said, rubbing his head, then stepping towards Tolomai.

"No!" cried Cathy, but the woman just laughed.

Then, her laugh turned into a shriek and, then, a scream, as Boots launched himself at her face with a piercing yowl, sinking claws into skin, causing her to stumble back through the doorway into the blazing building.

The men snapped out of their daze and hands released Cathy, only to seize her again as she rushed forward, after Boots and the woman.

"Whoa!" cried someone as they pulled her away from the flames.

The building collapsed with a roar and Cathy screamed.

The roar was followed by silence that was broken by a purr.

Cathy looked down. Boots, his fur a little singed, was at her feet. "Boots, you're alive!"

The cat jumped into her arms.

Tolomai stumbled awkwardly over and stroked it. "The little fellow roused me and saved my life."

Cathy looked around. The big man was gone.

Tolomai followed her gaze.

"We'll catch the villain," he said.

She looked back at the burning ruins. Unlike Boots, the woman hadn't emerged from the flames. It seemed as if the witch was no more.

"They were conspiring against the Prince," she told her uncle, when he came over to check on her. "Planning to kill him."

"Well," he said, observing the ruins of his business with a sigh, "let us hope he feels some gratitude at the foiling of the plot and pays to rebuild this place."

Cathy hoped so, too. But, most of all, she was just glad that everyone, and especially Boots, was alright.

She petted the cat and told him, "Thank you."

Boots nuzzled her cheek and purred in reply.

The Adventures of Colo Collins & Tama Toledo in Space and Time
By Tyree Campbell

Out on their first date, high school seniors Colo Collins and Tama Toledo are invited aboard a spaceship and offered the chance to intervene in various events in the Universe. These events can range from stopping an asteroid from striking a planet to helping someone find her house keys. But there's a catch: both Colo and Tama have to agree that an intervention should be performed . . . and sometimes they'll have to perform the intervention themselves!

Ordering Link:

https://www.hiraethsffh.com/product-page/adventures-of-colo-collins-tama-toledo-in-space-and-time-by-tyree-campbell

Before Plants
Jamie Manias

there were no herbivores —
only a living soup sipping itself
until it turned from broth
to brother. The first carnivore
had to be a cannibal
and cannibalism was a crime
of softness. Where
were the teeth? The sharp accessories?
Cannibals wore the softest skins of all.
So soft
they could slide another life under it
to dissolve, like a spa. Take its hat. Hang
its coat. Strip it with
tingling. Tongue the organelles
apart, no tears.

Space Station Zero-G
James Fitzsimmons

Dylan Crew motored his wheelchair into Space Station Zero-G. As the airlock closed behind him, Anita tousled his curly brown hair and kissed his forehead.

"Happy fourteenth birthday, Bro!"

"Yeah, yeah, Sis." Dylan loved seeing his big sister, but what really caught his attention was the statuesque blonde standing behind her. "Hi, Ms. Rose!"

Station Master Piper Rose smiled and shook his hand. "Good to see you again, Dylan. Call me Piper."

Absolutely, Dylan thought.

"You're just in time," Piper said. "Zero-g in five minutes."

Zero-g was when the wheel-shaped space station would stop rotating, and the one-Earth gravity that normally reigned over the inhabitants of the station would give way to weightlessness. Dylan loved experiencing zero-g, setting him free of his wheelchair and letting him float about the cabin.

"Last trip, you said you'd show me the control console, Piper," Dylan said, hoping she'd remember.

"Of course, Dylan—"

A page coming over the PA system interrupted Piper, asking for her attention.

She said to Dylan, "Come by the console when you're ready." She went to her position at the control console of the space station's bridge, where she monitored the thrusters on the outside of the structure.

Anita bent down and whispered into Dylan's ear: "You're fourteen and she's thirty. How's that going to work?"

"I really have no idea," he said, looking off with a smile.

"I have to get to the surgery bay," she said. "Mom's already there. See you in the break area after zero-g."

She punched his shoulder, and he watched her bound down a corridor like a gazelle. At seventeen, Anita was a prodigy who assisted their mother, Dr. Joyce Crew, in conducting surgical experiments in weightlessness on android models. This research would later be used to provide medical care to humans on long space missions. Dylan was proud of his mother and sister but wondered what his own life mission could be after the car crash three years ago that damaged his spinal cord and took away the use of his legs. The accident also took his father's life. Dylan lived with an uncle on Earth, and visited Joyce and Anita on the space station several times a year.

Now Dylan waited with anticipation until a warning siren announced the change in gravity, and others secured themselves into their workstations. The station accommodated fifty researchers along with a few super rich tourists who could afford to visit.

The gravity slowly subsided, and Dylan felt his body become light. He pushed himself out of his chair, grabbed a handhold on the wall, and, going from handhold to handhold, floated through the cabin toward Piper's console.

He stopped behind a steel girder when he saw Piper talking to Franklin Bates, the senior software engineer. Bates was a thin man who wore European cut suits and dress shirts with gold cuff links while most of the people onboard wore simple jumpsuits. Dylan could hear the tail end of Piper's and Bates' conversation.

". . . he's in the way, Piper. All I'm saying is wheelchairs belong on Earth, not in space."

Dylan saw them spot him, and they stopped talking. Then Bates adjusted his tie and returned to his workstation, using a tether. Dylan continued on to Piper's console.

"Sorry for Bates' poor manners," Piper said.

"My sister says Bates is jealous that my mom gets all the glory for the surgery project."

Piper tossed her head, causing her long blonde hair, secured with a pony tailer, to whip like a rope in slow motion. "He's in charge of the programming that operates the outside thrusters. Don't fret, he gets plenty of glory! And you're not in the way."

Dylan steadied himself over Piper's console and listened with fascination as

Piper explained the controls. There was a display that showed g-force, currently zero, one that showed rotations per minute, currently zero, and a touchscreen that allowed firing the thrusters.

"Most of this is run by computer," Piper said, "but we also need to be able to take manual control."

The weightlessness occurred twice a day, each session lasting an hour. When a session ended, the station would slowly begin rotating and the centrifugal force that the rotation produced would bring everyone back to one-g. As the session ended, Dylan softly came to a rest on the cabin floor. His wheelchair was a few meters away, and he summoned it to him with a remote, noticing Bates smirk as the chair rolled past him.

Dylan thanked Piper for the demo, then hoisted himself into the chair and went to meet Anita and his mom in the break area.

"Happy birthday, Dylan!" his mom and sister said, a triple chocolate cake waiting on a table.

"Hi, Mom," Dylan said, "thanks. Hey, what did Sis cut up today?"

"I removed an android's appendix," Anita said with a flourish of her arms.

"Did it live?" Dylan asked.

"Yes, Bro, it lived."

"How are your legs doing, Dylan?" Joyce asked.

Dylan had been undergoing spinal cord injections of stem cells taken from his bone marrow. The bone around the injury had been repaired after the accident, but no surgery could repair a damaged spinal cord. There was great hope that stem cells injected into the spine would stimulate the spinal nerves to regenerate.

Dylan shook his head. "Mom, the therapist pushes me, but I don't feel anything and can't move them."

His legs, uninjured in the accident, were kept in excellent shape thanks to electrodes that the physical therapist used to flex his legs, feet, and toes. But Dylan had lost hope he'd regain such control on his own.

"Keep working on it," Joyce said, hugging him.

After cake, Dylan and Anita shot baskets in the rec area, then Dylan got out of his chair and climbed onto a weightlifting machine. As he performed chest presses, Anita asked him to try some leg presses, but her prodding irritated him.

"I told you I can't, Anita. I'm sick of trying. I'm sick of that wheelchair. I've been in it for three years. I'm never going to—"

Dylan suddenly felt his body go light.

"Zero-g already?" he asked.

"Shouldn't be," Anita said.

The gravity slowly gave way to weightlessness, the warning siren sounded, and Piper's voice came over the PA system: "Attention! We're having an unscheduled session of zero-g. Sorry for the late notice."

Joyce hailed Piper on the intercom: "We don't have a medical procedure planned at this time."

"It's an error in the thruster software, Joyce. Bates is working on it now."

"Yippee!" Dylan said, pleased with the sudden weightlessness.

"Tell Bates to fix his programming!" Joyce said.

Dylan pushed up from the weight machine and quickly bumped his head into the ceiling. "Whoops!" he said, laughing, rubbing his head.

"Dylan! Careful!" Anita yelled.

Dylan pushed hard against the ceiling and shot back down, and, unable to slow himself, hit his lower back against the sharp metal edge of the weight machine.

"Ow!" Dylan yelled, feeling a sharp pain as his back arched.

"Dylan!" Joyce said. "Stay put!"

Joyce and Anita floated to Dylan, and Joyce observed Dylan's back while Anita held him still.

"Looks like you hit the area of your back near the original injury," Joyce said. "What do you think you're doing, Dylan?"

"I felt a crack," Dylan said, now moaning. "The pain is all over my back."

"Anita," Joyce said, "we need to address this now. If the repaired vertebra has broken, we can print a new one and install it."

"What!" Anita said.

Joyce floated to the intercom. "Piper, how long before we return to one-g?"

"No ETA, Joyce," Piper answered. "Bates says an hour at least."

"That's enough time. We're taking Dylan to surgery."

"What!"

Joyce quickly filled in Piper, then she and Anita floated Dylan to the surgery bay and secured him in a prone position to metal arms. In zero-g, a patient could be turned in any direction, and surgery could be approached from any angle.

Dylan was nervous as they turned him in multiple directions and took computerized scans of his back. His apprehension increased when his sister and mom donned masks and gloves, and a tray of surgical instruments suddenly appeared in midair.

"Sis, I'm not an android," he said, trying to calm himself.

"We haven't lost a patient yet," she said, but he thought he heard a tremor in her voice.

In minutes, Joyce was ready to administer anesthesia and said, "Dylan, count backwards from ten."

"Ten, nine, eight—"

***

When Dylan woke up in the recovery room, the last thing he remembered was counting down to eight.

"Hi, Bro," Anita said, tousling his hair.

"Hi, Sis. Feels like someone walked all over me. Is one-g back on?"

"Yep."

Joyce turned from a monitor and joined them. "Good work assisting, Anita. Dylan, we put in a new vertebra. The old one from three years ago was chipped, and the new ones are much improved. You'll be out of bed soon. Giving you some meds for the pain."

"Thanks, Mom."

"Son," Joyce continued, "when we removed the damaged bone and exposed the spinal cord, we took a micro-scan of the nerves. The area where the spinal cord was partly severed has repaired itself. It looks like your stem cell injections have regenerated nerve growth."

"You mean I'm cured? Why can't I walk?"

"We're not sure how the brain handles nerve regeneration. It could be you just need to keep working with your physical therapist. When you're having your sessions, tell yourself 'the connection is fixed,' because it is."

Bates and Piper entered the room.

"How are you doing, Dylan?" Piper asked.

Dylan shrugged and nodded, embarrassed that he got careless in zero-g.

Bates was silent, tugging on his collar and the sleeves of his jacket. Joyce motioned to Bates with her head, and she, Bates and Piper went outside into the hallway, but Dylan and Anita could hear them through the partly open door.

"What's with those thrusters?" Joyce asked.

"I think I have them corrected," Bates said.

"You think?"

"The software's complex, but it was a small bug."

"Small bug? My son needed immediate surgery."

"Your son shouldn't be on the station."

"Your software should work. You're lucky more people weren't hurt."

"Dr. Crew, I perform miracles every day, keeping this station stable. You're the one who had their budget increased at the last board meeting."

"Yes, now I get what you get, Mr. Bates."

"Guys, shhh!" Piper said.

Dylan heard footsteps retreat in opposite directions as Piper re-entered the room.

"Sorry, Dylan," Piper said. "Sometimes your mom and Bates have . . . words."

"They fight?" Dylan asked.

"It's more of a professional rivalry. Rest now."

"Piper, I think I'd like to pilot a station like this someday."

Piper smiled and exited.

"Pilot a station like this," Anita said in a mocking tone. "You're like a sick puppy around her."

Dylan smiled as Anita left, and then tried to sleep. But after a few minutes, he felt himself grow heavy and start to sink into the mattress. He sat up and swung himself into his wheelchair, but it took a lot of effort. At first, he thought he was sluggish from the painkillers, but then he heard people yelling for help outside his room. He found it difficult to turn the wheels of the chair and he switched on the motor.

In the hallway, people were sitting on the floor, some kneeling, some lying flat. He felt himself being pushed harder down into his chair. He headed off toward Piper's control console, and when he got near, he saw Bates on his stomach, trying to crawl along the floor by pulling on footholds.

Then Dylan gasped when he saw Piper behind her console, her foot caught in a foothold and twisted.

"Dylan!" Piper yelled. "Can you make it to the control panel?"

Dylan applied more power to his chair. The motor whined and the chair moved slowly.

"The station is taking several g's!" Piper yelled. "Bates can't make it to the console. My foot is caught."

Dylan was able to motor to the console, but Piper's stool was blocking the way. Dylan could hear Piper cry out in pain, and he rammed the stool with his wheelchair and kicked it with both legs at the same time. The stool scooted a few inches, and he kicked it again. Now he was in front of the console, but the control panel was above his head. He pushed a button on the arm of the wheelchair, and the seat raised him high enough to reach the panel.

"Piper! What do I do now!"

Piper yelled some commands, and he entered them on a keyboard. She yelled more instructions, and he tapped them on the touchscreen. As the centrifugal force began to slowly decrease, he felt the heavy weight being lifted from his body and saw the g-force reading on the console return to one-Earth gravity.

Bates got up and ran to the console.

"Thanks, Dylan, well done."

Dylan motored to Piper, who was sitting up and rubbing her foot.

"Thank goodness, Dylan," she said. "I see the software still has a few bugs."

Anita and Joyce ran up to the console, and Joyce bent down to examine Piper's foot.

"We were in the surgery bay but couldn't get out," Anita said.

"Dylan saved us," Piper said. "Dylan, you used your legs to push away my stool."

Joyce and Anita looked sharply at Dylan.

"Huh!" Dylan said.

***

Over the next couple of days, Dylan worked with Anita in the rec area, taking small steps with the help of a cane. He became strong enough to shoot baskets while standing and to do leg presses. He worked hard to steady himself and maintain balance. He even wondered if at some point he dare try out for high school basketball, a dream he'd given up hope on.

But the time to leave the station came all too soon for Dylan, and he was now walking to the ferry for his return to Earth.

Joyce and Piper met him at the airlock, Piper herself walking with a cane.

"Dylan," Piper said, "your progress is remarkable. I'm still healing from my ankle twist. You're now my first mate."

If only that were true, Dylan thought. He motioned to Bates hunched over his workstation, his head bowed as if deep in thought. The software engineer had taken to wearing a jumpsuit in place of a dress suit. "What about Mr. Bates?"

"The space station board is conducting a full investigation," Piper said.

Dylan saw Anita bounding down the corridor toward them, and said in a soft voice but loud enough for her to hear, "Well, Mr. Bates doesn't have a genius helping him."

Anita smiled.

"We'll be down in a few months, Son," Joyce said, "when we take a break from the project. Keep working with your physical therapist." She kissed him.

Then Dylan passed through the airlock into the ferry.

"Wait!" Anita yelled and ran into the ferry. She started crying, hugged him, and tousled his hair. "I have to reach up now," she said. She wiped her eyes and returned to the station.

"See ya, Sis," Dylan said, summoning his wheelchair, which followed him into the ferry. He waved as the airlock closed. He was sad to leave Space Station Zero-G, but was happy to walk back to Earth.

The Field Trip
Ellie Murphy - Sixth Grade

I HATE museums. They're so boring, and of course, because I have bad luck, MY class is going on a field trip to a stupid *nature* museum. I don't like nature. It's so humid, buggy, and gross. I'd rather stay inside, play video games, and eat chips.

Yesterday we got our field trip buddies. I'm lucky I got paired with my best friend James. I'm grateful that I got paired with James, but I think it's just a bit odd. I usually get paired up with this boy named Titus Claussen, he's the MOST ANNOYING kid in the whole school. Because of my bad luck, he's in three of my classes and I always get paired with him, but not this time!

I got paired up with the new girl too. Ugh.

There was assigned seating on the bus, as usual. I don't know why everybody was so sad that they didn't get to choose their seats. We never get to choose our seats on field trips. James is two rows behind me. I had to sit next to the new girl, which isn't bad, I just don't like interacting with people (except for James of course).

"Hi. Lucy, right?" the new girl says.

I pretend not to notice, I don't want to talk, I'm not in the mood.

"Uh, hello? Girly pops!"

I have no choice but to answer. Ugh. "What did you say? Sorry, I was zoned out," I lie.

"Oh, I was just asking if your name was Lucy," she says.

"Oh yeah! Haha! How'd you know?" I pretend to be interested, it's torture.

"You were at the science fair. I saw your project. It was really good."

"Wow, thanks! What's your name?" I say, trying to be polite.

"Samantha. But, you can call me Sam if you want." Sam seems a bit needy for friends but she's nice. Sometimes I see her walking alone in the halls. I never paid much attention. "Are you excited for the field trip?! I LOVE nature! Did you know that bees DANCE to communica-"

I cut her off. "You talk a LOT."

"Oh sorry. Nobody has ever talked to me before."

"No, I'm not excited for the field trip," I say.

"Really? Why?" Sam says.

"Because, I hate nature."

"Oh that's sad. Uh...uh..um..do you like cats?" Sam says.

"I'm more of a dog person, but...um ... yeah," I say.

"Cool. So, what's your thing?"

"Umm, my thing? Sam, you got to be more specific."

"Like, what are you good at? What do you like?"

"Oh! I like video games, chips, anime... yeah that's it."

The conversation trailed off after that. I was glad the conversation was over but what I didn't like was how awkward it was. I'm almost positive Sam was uncomfortable too. That was the longest bus ride I've ever had. I look behind me and spot James talking to the person next to him. James knows everyone and everyone knows him but he's not popular or unpopular, he's in the middle. I'm in the middle too, well sort of, I'm more unpopular. Okay I lied, I'm unpopular.

"Alright, everybody get with your buddies. We are heading into the museum," the teacher says as I get up from my seat and go over to James. Sam follows, which at first I thought was weird until I realized that she was in our group. Darn.
"All alright everyone! My name is Austin and I'll be your guide." He was a slim man with short brown hair. He wore overalls with a plaid shirt under it. The overalls looked like Mount Everest compared to a human. The museum tour guide told us about all the photos and paintings, "and this one about how the artist would sit on a rock and stare out into the distance." the tour guide says.

As we enter the next exhibit James whispers to me, "Lucy! Are you bored too?"

"Yeah. now, shhhh!" I whisper.

The tour guide repeated the same thing over and over: he would walk to a painting or a photo, we would crowd around and he would say, "And this one's about blank." Seriously I think he's trying too hard.

Finally! Lunch! We eat in the cafeteria.

As usual, James and I sit together.

"So James, who were you talking to on the bus?"

"This guy named Matt. He's cool," James says. "Hey, you were talking to Sam, the new girl right? The one in our group? She's sitting there all alone. We should invite her over to our table!" James says as he starts to get up from his chair.

"What? No!" I say, stopping him by the shirt.

"Why not?"

"Because we...were...uh talking! Yeah!" I say letting him go. "We weren't talking! We were sitting there in silence!"

Before I can argue he walks over to where Sam is sitting. Before I can decide if I want to stop James, Sam is already over to me. I stand there for a while thinking, until I sit down.

"So Sam, what's that you're eating?" James says.

"Oh, this? It's a mustard and ham sandwich"

"Ew," I say.

"Lucy! Don't be rude!" James says.

"Whatever," I say

After lunch, our teacher told us to get together with our buddies and explore any exhibit we'd like. We just had to meet back in the cafeteria in twenty minutes.

"Who's going to set the timer? James?"

"Nah I forgot my watch at home."

"Lucy?"

"Uh hehe. Nope. Don't have a watch. But you do" I say pointing at Sam's watch....

"Oh yeah!"

"Hey guys! We should go to the exotic animals exhibit!" James says.

"Oooh! That looks cool!" Sam agrees with James.

James and Sam speed walk over to the exhibit entrance.

"Hey, Lucy! Come on!" Sam says.

I groan and walk towards the entrance of the exotic animals exhibit.

"Oooo! Look at that one with the giant spider!" James says.

"Cool!" Sam says.

This exhibit is super cool, but I don't admit it.

"Uuuugh! This is so lame!" I complain.

"Alright, Lucy stop! I am tired of you complaining about everything!" Sam says.

I lean against the wall, near a painting of a tiger with the talons and wings of an eagle and the teeth of a shark. "Jeez," I say.

"Beeeeeeeep!"

"What was that?" James asks.

"My watch! It's glowing!"

James and I stare at Sam's watch with wide eyes, Sam's watch lifts up from her arm rising three feet in the air.

"**Look at the top of the watch! The hands are gone!**" I yell.

I look to the side and see one of the paintings glowing too! Suddenly there's a bright light! We cover our eyes, and then...... black.

I wake up on a beach, Sam and James are up too. I get up and look out to sea, which you expect to be a huge ocean right? Nope. It's a giant painting that moves well, not the painting itself but what's in it. People in the painting move around pointing at different things in the room. It takes me a little while to notice, "Hey! That's where we were!" I scream.

Sam and James jump up from the ground and run over to where I am standing.

"I said, that's where we were!"

"Yeah. We heard you the first time" Sam says.

"Wait! I got an idea!" James says stepping backwards and then bolting towards the painting. It pushes him off with a big glob noise. James skids back, gets up, and tries again, and again, and again. Sam and I stand there, a little concerned for James.

"It's no use, you have to go to the other side."

James stops, we spin around and see a tall boy with short dark hair cargo pants and a stained T-shirt.

"Who are you?" Sam asks.

"Hugo. What's your name?" Hugo says.

"Uhh, I'm Sam and this is Lucy and James."

"Hi," James and I say together.

"Come I'll show you guys the way!" Hugo says.

"Okay! Thanks!" James says.

"Yeah, let's go!" Sam says.

I jump in front of them. "We don't even know if we can trust Hugo," I whisper.

"Of course we can! His name is Hugo!" James says.

They push past me, and I follow.

"Oh! My watch!" Sam says picking it up and latching it on her arm.

"So, Hugo, what's this about the other side?" James says.

"Ah! Excellent question!" Hugo answers. "So this is a magical land that only certain people can visit. So first, congrats! You're one of those people!"

"I don't believe this! It's insane! A magical land! I am dreaming. Pinch me." I say.

"Shh! The master is speaking!" James says, bowing to Hugo.

"Thanks, James. So as I was saying, you are one of those people! So I've been here for a long time! A month maybe? But the thing is, a year here is an hour in the mortal land."

"Wait, wait, wait, so you're saying we're IMMORTAL! Cool!" Sam says.

"No! Here we aren't immortal, we refer to those on Earth as mortal because they don't know about this place. Anyway, if you are wondering if people saw you transfer here, they didn't. it's like you weren't even in the exhibit! We have to be careful, there are dangerous mythical creatures."

Just then we hear a deep growl. The creature is a tiger with the talons and wings of an eagle, and the teeth of a shark, Hugo pulled out his sword which I didn't even notice!

Sam, James, and I all hide in a bush while leaving Hugo to the monster. Hugo draws his sword back preparing to stab the monster straight through the heart. The monster opens its mouth revealing two things: Shiny white teeth, and a large roar! Hugo backs up past our hiding bush. He bolts forward, sliding under the monster and stabbing his sword into the monster's stomach. The monster stumbles, falling with a large "thud!" Hugo climbs up onto the monster and stabs it right through the heart. The monster lets out one last painful roar. It's dead. The thing that amazes me is that Hugo did this all in complete silence. No grunting or even a drop of sweat as he casually jumps off the monster's stomach.

"Come on guys! No time to waste!" Hugo says as if nothing happened. "Now, where was I? Ah! Yes mythical creatures, so there are a bunch of mythical creatures, so watch your back! But anyway, the other side is another painting, the same as the one you came in through but, instead of sucking you IN, it spits you OUT." Hugo says.

"So you're saying that we have to walk all the way over to the OTHER side to get out!? That's insane!" I say.

"Yup! Looks like you've got the jist!" Hugo replies. "Oh yeah...forgot to mention, there are a bunch of evil people. That is kinda, sorta, trying to kill me. So we gotta watch out for them." Hugo says.

"WHAT!? So NOW we have to be prepared for mythical creatures AND evil people!? I hate this place." I say.

An hour passes. No mystical creatures or evil people, whew.

We hear rapid footsteps that seem to be getting close.

Hugo looks behind us, "RUN!" Hugo screams.

I supposed that everyone's instinct is to run. Including mine. But before I run I look behind me to see about ten men bolting towards us. They have black goo streaked across their cheeks and rags with a lot of weapons. Noticing this I do what any normal human would do: Scream at the top of their lungs and run for their life. I bolt faster than ever in my life. I run past James, Sam, and Hugo. Sam and James look surprised. Both have seen me run track in gym class and within thirty seconds I would collapse from exhaustion. But this is different. MY life is being threatened. The evil people are gaining on us.

"They're gaining on us!" Sam says, gasping for breath.

"Ya don't think I noticed?" I say.

"Quick turn!" Hugo says, turning a sharp corner leading to thick bushes. We duck behind the thick bushes. The evil people run past us.

"Who are those people?" Sam whispers gasping for breath as quietly as she can.

"They call themselves *the E.P.,*" Hugo says.

"Why the *E.P.?* Does it stand for something?" James asks.

"It stands for evil people," Hugo says.

"Wow, real creative," I say sarcastically.

"Shhhhhhhhh!"

"Sorry!" I whisper.

But it is too late. I hear footsteps coming closer. Suddenly, I see them. They are huge and look ready to rip anyone in half. We get up and run. We rush through the trees, practically flying. At this point we don't care where we are going as long as we get away from the E.P. I am dodging trees and jumping over fallen trees. Leaves are crunching aggressively with every step.

In the distance, we see a beach!

"Look! Is that the other side?!" Sam says.

"Yup. sure is. Now when we get there, run as fast as you can towards the painting." Hugo says.

"You sure?" I say.

"Positive," Hugo says.

The painting gets closer and closer until I'm running on sand. We all pick up the pace, running even faster, and we brace ourselves...we are in some sort of transition place because there are swirling colors around us forming a tube. It's beautiful. We find ourselves back at the front of the museum.

"Wow," James says.

"Yeah," Sam says.

"Well, I guess this is goodbye," Hugo says.

"Wait! Dude, you can't leave without giving me your phone number!" James says.

"Okay. Here," Hugo says, giving James his phone number.

"Oh, guys! We gotta be back at the cafeteria in five minutes!" Sam says, looking at her watch.

"Wait, I have one last question for you Hugo. If you knew about the other portal, why didn't you leave earlier?" I ask.

"Well, that's true. I did know about the other portal, but it didn't feel like the right time to leave," Hugo answers. "Oh! I gotta meet my parents in fifteen minutes! Bye! Text me!" Hugo says.

We go to the cafeteria, just in time.

It turns out that this museum isn't as bad as I thought, but I don't admit it.

Aliens, Magic, and Monsters
By Lauren McBride

Fun to read. Fun to write. *Aliens, Magic, and Monsters* features poems set in the unlimited and imaginative realm of science fiction, fantasy, and horror. The poems were chosen to showcase over twenty poetic forms from acrostiku to zip, from strict rhyme to free verse, and much more in between. There are guidelines included on how to write each type of poem. Try a sci(na)ku. At only six words, it's sure to interest even the youngest readers.

Type: Juvenile and Young Adult Poetry Manual
Ordering links:
Print: https://www.hiraethsffh.com/product-page/aliens-magic-and-monsters-by-lauren-mcbride

ePub: https://www.hiraethsffh.com/product-page/aliens-magic-and-monsters-by-lauren-mcbride-2

PDF: https://www.hiraethsffh.com/product-page/aliens-magic-and-monsters-by-lauren-mcbride-1

Thaw
Alex McNall

Gemma stares into the mist, searching for something, *anything*, in the cold gray fog.

Her room's on the south side, facing the sun hovering above the hazy horizon. Thick glass chills her cheek, but her body is burning up, even without a coat. Nobody knows she sleeps on top of the covers, conditioning for the cold.

"The only things out there are ice and death."

Gemma spins from the window to face her uncle, Grayson.

"Mom wouldn't have left if there wasn't a reason," Gemma says.

"She went outside because she lost her mind." Grayson removes one glove to stroke his white, wispy beard. "She wasn't the first."

"At least she did *something*." Gemma stands to meet his tired eyes. "We won't make it through another winter."

"We will make it as long as we have to," he replies. "When the thaw comes, all the sacrifices will have been worth it."

"Then I better go water the potatoes." Gemma pushes past her uncle.

"Yes, you better," he says. "And put on your coat."

***

Gemma cuts a knobby tuber and plants the pieces, covers them with compost made of human waste. She sprinkles water and positions the lamps.

Even if the little sprouts worm their way up to catch the light, Gemma won't be around to see them. She'll also miss the bloom of sickly white buds, the only flowers she's ever known. Her grandmother spoke of red ones, blue ones, even yellow ones brighter than the sun.

Her *great*-grandmother was a child when the rocks fell from the sky, saw cloudless days hot enough to burn the skin. Then the meteors kicked up a cloud that blotted out the sun. The only hope they've ever had is that one day the thaw will come.

Gemma's mother got tired of waiting.

"The stars are wrong," she would say, watching through windows on rare cloudless nights. "How can the stars be wrong?"

The lights in the night once helped people navigate, stellar guideposts. Gemma only needs to know one direction—south.

The week's harvest makes thin soup spread among twelve adults, three children, and a baby. As the group gathers to eat, Gemma sneaks away.

"Where are you going?" Grayson asks, stepping from his office.

"Left something in the nursery." Gemma goes to a door labeled stairs, picks the lock with a sewing needle.

She sparks a lighter and makes a quick descent. The last few drops of fuel won't last long. She's explored eight levels of the underground compound, which once held hundreds waiting out the winter.

She discovered a window on the fourth floor, breaking glass to feel the exposed rock beyond. It was cold, hard, and slick to the touch.

Ice.

Because they aren't underground, just buried under tons of snow. The community lives on the top floor, only hope of escape through the roof. She scavenges abandoned areas, taking equipment from a time when people ventured outside. Gemma still needs skis to go with her boots and poles.

She scours another room, finding useless computers and electronics. The lighter flickers.

"Not yet..." she trots down a narrow hall.

The flame dies and darkness swallows her. The full weight of the place, generations of death and despair, settle upon her. She trips on something, kneecaps striking concrete.

"Ow!" Gemma hears another voice and freezes.

Ow ow ow...

No, just an echo. It's too cold for ghosts.

She gropes along the floor and feels the things that tripped her—skis. Gemma beams in the blackness, then finds the stairs and rushes toward the pinhole of light.

***

The final necessity is a pack of strike-anywheres. Gemma breaks into her uncle's office and rummages the cabinets. She finds the matches and bumps something, knocking it to the floor. A globe. She sets it upright and notices the crooked axis for the first time. Was it always so tilted?

Her mother's words echo in her head.

The stars are wrong.

But if stars don't move, then the planet must be wrong. It all falls into place as the door bursts open.

"You're going in the cell," Grayson says, flanked by two nephews.

"But there could be green lands to the south," Gemma says.

"The thaw will come here. This was a green land."

"We're not where you think we are, uncle." Gemma kicks the globe. "This land will never thaw if the meteors moved the Earth!"

"If we leave, we die," Grayson says.

"I rather die quickly out there," she says, "than slowly in here."

"It's not up to you."

The men advance and Gemma lunges for the door. Grayson grabs her, but she rips one arm free, overpowering malnourished muscles and stabbing him with the needle. She sprints to the roof, grabbing her stash on the stairs. Six hatchet hits break the boards that block the door.

Gemma shoulders her pack and clicks into the skis. "I will return," she whispers to the wind. "I promise."

She pushes off and slides down a snow bank as Grayson's shouts are lost in the fog.

Gemma falls on the crunchy boilerplate many times, finding her balance. When the wind picks up, she unfurls the bed sheet tied to her coat. The sail pulls her south with surprising speed.

She only stops to eat and sleep, even as fingertips turn black. Days of icy valleys and snowy hills stretching to infinity. On the morning of the thirteenth day, Gemma collapses and hits something hard.

Rock—exposed and basking in the sun.

She follows dark patches of stone like footprints in the snow. They led to a valley where a trickle carves its way between the rocks.

"Water!"

Gemma laps at the creek, then looks up to see smoky rivers pouring into the sky. The columns rise from buildings jutting from the ice like bones. One is impossibly tall, a needle stabbing at the stars. She cries, hot tears freeing a sprout springing from the earth.

A yellow flower, brighter than the sun.

Who?

Lydia Volokh is 12 years old and lives in Atlanta, Georgia, with her dog, three cats, and some human family members. In addition to writing, Lydia loves reading, portrait drawing, and cooking.

Ellie Murphy started writing various stories as soon as she could hold a pencil. She lives among two sisters, two parents, and a rather amazing dog. Ellie wrote "The Field Trip" as part of a creative writing club at her school, Midtown International School.

Barbara Candiotti is an artist and writer who traverses the Science Fiction, Horror, and Fantasy genres. She lives with two talkative senior cats in the Pacific Northwest, where sparkling waters and lush greenery provide daily inspiration.

Lisa Timpf's speculative poetry has appeared in a variety of magazines and anthologies. When not writing, Lisa enjoys organic gardening, bird-watching, and walking her lively Jack Russel-cocker spaniel Chet. You can find out more about Lisa's writing at http://lisatimpf.blogspot.com/.

Michelle St. James is a published author and artist, whose artwork has appeared in a variety of publications. Her YA novel, <u>The Mermaid of Agawam Bay</u>, is available on Amazon. Check out more of her art on www.stjames-art.com

All things are connected. That's the premise of what **William J. Joel** does. Each of Mr. Joel's interests informs each other. Mr. Joel has been teaching computer science since 1983 and has been a writer even longer.

William Shaw is a writer from Sheffield, currently living in the USA. You can find his website at
https://williamshawwriter.wordpress.com
and his Bluesky at
@williamshaw.bsky.social.

DJ Tyrer lives near the world's longest pleasure pier in the decaying seaside resort of Southend-on-Sea, is the person behind Atlantean Publishing, and has been published in a variety of anthologies and magazines

James Fitzsimmons writes sf, fantasy, and horror. He loves writing for youth, when the senses of wonder and adventure are at their peak!

Alex McNall grew up adventuring in the woods, relying on his imagination to keep himself entertained. He may never have super powers, travel through time, or go to outer space, so instead he writes about it. He's based in the SF Bay Area and enjoys interacting with his backyard squirrels.

Lauren McBride is author of the chapbook *Aliens, Magic, and Monsters* (Hiraeth, 2023). Nominated for the Best of the Net, Pushcart, Rhysling, and Dwarf Stars Awards, her poetry has appeared internationally. She enjoys swimming, gardening, baking, reading, writing, and knitting scarves for U.S. troops.

Greer Woodward's science fiction and fantasy poems have appeared in Illumen, Scifaikuest, Star*Line, and Silver Blade. Along with Adele Gardner, Greer edited the 2022 Dwarf Stars Anthology, She lives on the Big Island of Hawaii with her husband, actor John Sucke, and six cats.

Jamie Manias is a poet and teacher at Bowling Green State University, as well as an assistant editor for Mid-American Review. They are made of trillions of cells and so are you. Their poems can be found in Kingfisher Magazine, The Amazine, and dadakuku and other publications.

Brian Rosenberger lives in a cellar in Marietta, GA and writes by the light of captured fireflies. He is the author of As the Worm Turns and three poetry collections - Poems That Go Splat, And For My Next Trick..., and Scream for Me.

Guy Belleranti writes fiction, non-fiction, poetry, puzzles and humor for both children and adults. He worked for many years in school libraries. He is also a long-time docent educator at the local zoo. His author's website is http://guy-belleranti.weebly.com/

www.ingramcontent.com/pod-product-compliance
Lightning Source LLC
LaVergne TN
LVHW012033060526
838201LV00061B/4575